ALGECIRAS

As he drove away his mind was flashing through the fights they'd had. It seemed like their whole life had been a battle. He'd got to the point of leaving several times before but she'd always managed to talk him round.

He drove on. Round a roundabout, down to the traffic lights in the high street. Carefully, methodically... He looked in his wallet, no money, bloody marvellous.

He pulled up outside a bank and took two hundred pounds from the machine. He tried again but it refused. He cussed and drove off.

Not really knowing why, he drove to the airport. Maybe it was because he knew the bar would be open.

After a few hours heavy drinking he found himself standing at the ticket desk. His eyes blurred as he stared at the destination board. He wasn't quite sure where he was going but he knew he had to go.

"Next flight to Gibraltar boarding at bay six." The announcement startled him.

"Gibraltar," he said.

"Certainly sir, card, cheque or cash?"

"Card,"he replied fumbling with his wallet and his thoughts.

He wondered for a minute what was going on but gave up.

" Go with the flow, " he muttered to himself and wandered off to find bay six.

As he sat on the plane, more memories from the past came flooding back to haunt him. His job, what was he going to do about his job. Maybe he could ring them tomorrow and get a few weeks off, just so he could get things sorted out.

But he knew it wouldn't sort out. He had a few more drinks to forget his problems.

He woke up with a jolt as the plane landed at Gibraltar and fumbled around for his luggage only to realise he didn't have any. He followed the other passengers off the plane and through customs, his brain bleary with the sleep and the drink.

The other passengers either got into waiting cars or taxis or were greeted lovingly by family or friends. He turned away from the lights and towards the bus terminal where he followed a few people on to a bus. He thought it might be a holiday bus but it wasn't. No happy faces here he thought, only the tired and the weary.

He had no idea where he was going. No suitcase, only his wallet and a few bank cards.

The front of the bus said "ALGECIRAS" but he didn't know and he didn't care either.

He fell asleep again as the bus crossed the border into southern Spain. He awoke to find the bus stationary in a side street. Only a few people were left on the bus and they were slowly shuffling forward to get off.

He stood up, his eyes tired as he tried to make out the buildings in the street. He wondered if he was still dreaming. People were speaking in Spanish, he looked at them and wondered where he was. He stopped wondering, the pain was too much.

He saw the lights of a bar beckoning and he followed them.

It was half dark inside the bar. A T.V. set blared out from the corner, it's flickering screen illuminating the faces of the Spanish men seated around it.

"Beer", he said, slouching on to a bar stool, his arms leaning heavily on the bar, "and a bottle of navy rum". The barman didn't understand.

"Rum", he repeated pointing, "and a bottle of coke", he pointed again.

The barman opened a fresh bottle of rum for him, Lamb's Navy, his favourite and put the bottle of coke beside it. He looked round the bar for Glen's companions but there were none. He took a glass from below the counter, Glen signalled for a larger one.

"Two thousand pesetas", the barman said.

Glen looked at his purchases. "Cigarettes", he pointed along the back shelf to the Benson and Hedges. At least he wouldn't have to suffer the Spanish cigarettes.

It was then that he realised that he didn't have any Spanish money. Starting to feel rather nervous and stupid he pulled out his wallet and offered a credit card.

"No", said the barman looking at him in a chilling kind of way. The locals at the other end of the room started to shuffle a bit as they sensed an atmosphere of confrontation.

Glen pulled out a twenty pound note and offered it to the barman.

"Ci"

The locals settled back to their T.V. programme and the

barman passed over the change in pesetas. It certainly didn't look like much change but Glen was past caring. He drank half the beer straight down, grabbed the ice box and half filled the other glass with ice. He poured the rum in and sipped it neat. Lighting a cigarette he turned around on his stool to find a more comfortable seat.

He took the beer, the rum and coke to a seat in the corner shadows, obscured from the other patrons.

He sat there all night drinking and smoking.

Anything to stop from thinking.

*

Chapter 1

It was morning. The sky was clear blue, the sun hanging low in the early morning sky, pale yet brilliant.

The mediterranean sea glistened below, the waves rolling along the beach into the distance.

The dusty main street where the bar stood had one or two occasional passers by. A car lifted the dust as it noisily chugged on it's way and a cyclist who couldn't ride very well zig - zagged past.

The front of the bar had a veranda with a few tables and chairs, a sofa with a crumpled figure on it left over from the previous nights excesses.

He turned slowly over and then resettled, continuing to sleep.

Following the trail of dust left by the car you could see the white glistening sands of the beach, the waves gently falling into a misty spray.

This was Algeciras, the outskirts of the sleepy Spanish town that Glen had run to.

Nobody took much notice of him as he lay there.

He slept 'til past noon. The bar opened, customers came and went. They even sat at the tables beside him but they still took no notice.

He finally woke up in the late afternoon.

His eyes opened, strained against the sun. He wondered where he was and closed them again, he didn't want to know.

The pain swelled up inside his stomach and he looked around for a bottle.

And so the days and nights passed. The barman rented him a room upstairs as an alternative to sleeping rough but he continued to drink away the days and nights.

He heard a noise, it sounded familiar, something in his

mind began to rattle.

"How's it going then sunshine?"

The words and the lips moved in a way he couldn't quite comprehend.

He saw the lips, he heard the words. The face looked at him, pausing a while, waiting for a response.

"I shall....." , Glen spoke,"I shall......", his throat was rough and caused him to choke into a cough. "I have to phone the office." He eventually managed to get the words out.

"This is the office mate, there's only one place to do business and this is it."

He stopped and looked at Glen who was swaying slightly from side to side even though he was seated at the bar.

"If you want insurance, a house, a carpenter or a plumber this is where you'll find it."

It was late evening and Glen was well into his usual routine of mellow - mindlessness.

The Guardia walked into the bar and the locals went suddenly very quiet. They talked in a whisper to the barman and looked at the two Englishmen who were trying their best to look inconspicuous.

"Don't walk around the streets drunk will you," the Englishman whispered to Glen, "they're partial to cracking drunks with their batons."

Glen looked at him quizzically trying to focus on the person in front of him.

"How about a drink then?" The rallying cry of a dedicated enthusiast.

"Don't mind if I do", the Englishman smiled and lifted his glass in salute.

They got to talking. The Englishman's name was Harry, he claimed to be a builder but Glen assumed that really he only organised other people to do work for the ex - pats.

"Do you want a job then Glen?" Harry enquired, "I've

got plenty of things that you could do."

"I've got a job thanks." Glen didn't seem quite sure.

"What's that then?" Harry looked again at the saggy mess in front of him.

"I'm a system's analyst, Harry." Glen wasn't quite sure if he'd managed to say it without slurring but he'd tried his best.

Harry picked up his drink and looked thoughtful for a while.

"Oh that's very handy," he said sarcastically, "that's just what we need around here, a system's analyst."

"I must ring the office."

He woke up in the usual bleary stupor.

"I must ring the office," he thought, "they must be going mad."

He ran a full bath and soaked for a good hour before he could bring himself to face another day.

"I must ring the kids and see that they're alright."

He shaved and then spoke on the phone to Sasha and Jake at length. He tried to explain that he was having a break and he'd keep in touch but it wasn't easy.

"I must ring the office."

Eventually he did.

He saw Harry again that evening in the bar. They were chatting together when Glen was distracted by the entrance of a woman he had not seen before.

She talked briefly to the barman and then turned and looked straight at Glen. Glen held her gaze, unabashed that he might be staring. She turned from the bar and walked slowly towards him still holding his gaze.

Harry's words drifted on and over his head as his mind fully appreciated her every movement. Every step, every slight tilt of the shoulder, the sway of the dress over her body. "Yes," he thought, "this is it, this is my time."

She arrived at the table still staring straight into Glen's eyes and he into hers. He found himself suddenly lost for words.

She sat down opposite Glen and without averting her eyes spoke to Harry, who by now had realised that he had lost Glen's attention.

"Harry?" she spoke slowly with a hushed deep tone.

"When are you going to get someone to finish my decorating?"

Glen's mind fractured into a million pieces.

"Why the fuck is she talking to Harry. Why isn't she

talking to me to me?" he raged to himself.

He pondered the squareness of her jaw and the rise of her high cheek bones. His eyes trailed to her lips, her teeth and then he realised. He realised he was too pissed to speak and was gloating like a drunk over a rare jewel.

She stood up and walked away.

What had Harry said? Why had she gone?

He watched in torture as she left the bar and then sat in a bemused silence.

Harry spoke first.

"You sure you don't want to do some decorating?"

Glen smiled and they broke into a laugh.

"I'll drink to that."

Another brilliant sunny morning.

Glen met Harry in the bar for an early breakfast. Ten o'clock is relatively early in Spain where the peak of the day is spent in cool siesta's and work is more of a diversion than an occupation.

They drove slowly to the edge of town to find Louise Darcy's house. Up the winding road which snaked up the hillside and in through the front gate.

"It's a breathtaking view," Glen said to Harry who was having trouble getting out of the jeep.

They stood together for a few minutes taking in the landscape. The hills rolling down to the sand dunes and the piercing blue sea. The ships in the harbour shining brilliant white in the glare of the sun. The streets of the town below and on the horizon out to sea the Rock of Gibraltar the last piece of old England left in the mediterranean.

"It's a hard life ," said Harry sardonically as he shuffled his way up the drive, "but someone's got to do it."

Glen just smiled, he was slightly overawed by the beauty of the panoramic view and even more so when he turned to see the opulence of the house.

It was all a long way from his modest little semi in England.

They walked up the drive and on to the path which led them through an ornately laid garden.

Louise Darcy was lying on a sun lounger on the hacienda at the front of the house. The white decked arches seemed to go all round the outside, perhaps they did.

Louise didn't move or greet them as they stepped on to the hacienda beside her.

"Have a seat," she said casually from below the brim of her sun hat which was tilted down obscuring most of her face. "I'll be with you in a minute."

Glen took the opportunity to appreciate her athletic build. She wore shorts and a skimpy vest which covered the minimum.

Harry phased off into a daydream staring intently at some unknown point on the horizon.

Glen started to think again about his wife and children in England and the reason for his hurried departure.

He shivered.

Louise stood up. "The paint's in the garage and here's the colour scheme for the lounge." She walked off into the house holding out a piece of paper. They both followed.

"Help yourself to tea and coffee, I'm off to town."

She drove off with Glen and Harry watching the dust swirling on the drive.

Harry left shortly after, leaving Glen to wander the house.

He eventually settled in the kitchen and started the days work with a long tea break.

Glen finished rollering the walls and then headed for the beach.

He was hot and sweaty and couldn't wait to freshen up in the sea.

He threw his t-shirt and shoes on to the sand and walked straight into the sea in his boxer shorts.

He swam through the breaking surf and out into the calm beyond. He swam as hard as he could, the muscles in his arms and legs straining, stretching himself to feel the power within and from the sea. He swam below the surface opening his eyes, he was amazed how clear the water, the small fish darting about, the crabs scuffling along and the flounders trying to conceal themselves in the sand. It felt so good, so clean, so pure, so free.

He suddenly realised he **was** free, free from all the pain and suffering he had endured for years in a destructive marriage

He lay on his back, savouring the moment, floating. His mind free clear and untroubled.

For half an hour he must have stayed there daydreaming, then he made his way back to the beach.

Picking up his shoes and using the shirt to dry himself off, he walked up the beach to the back of a bar.

He ordered a pizza, a beer and picked out a table with an umbrella sun shade. He sat a while pondering the view as he drank.

"With this weather it's difficult to get anyone to work for long."

He felt a soft hand on his shoulder. It was Louise Darcy standing behind him.

Her voice had a deep calm about it that Glen liked.

He half turned towards her,"I did a couple of walls before it got too hot."

"I see you've cooled off now," she replied looking at his soaking wet shorts which were clinging to his thighs in a revealing way.

Glen's pizza arrived so he ordered a drink and a pizza for

Louise.

He looked at her as she sank back into the chair, relaxed and tanned, he couldn't quite believe his luck.

They spent the next few hours chatting and bantering as if they'd known each other for years. They bought a jug of Sangria and moved to the sun beds on the beach.

Louise decided to sunbathe topless and removed her vest.

Glen, who hadn't quite perfected the art of looking a topless woman in the eyes whilst conversing, was lost for words for a while.

The sangria began to work it's merry way around their thoughts. They looked at each other and laughed, their heads falling together in a drunken giggle.

"I'm sorry," said Glen apologetically, "I'm afraid I'm a bit of a basic kind of guy. When a woman flashes her boobs, I've just got to go for it."

Louise dissolved into hysterical giggles moving toward him as if to speak. He lent over to listen but she kissed him gently on the cheek. As he turned their lips met, brushing each other teasingly.

The teasing led to more earnest kissing, then they couldn't stop kissing or laughing.

Aware that they were about to exceed the boundaries of social decency they got up to leave. The adrenalin rushing through their bodies they made their way arm in arm.

"Your place or mine," said Glen.

"Both," said Louise.

Algeciras 3, page 9.

They bought another jug of Sangria from the bar below Glen's flat and retired.

Louise set up the glasses and removed her top again. " What was that you said about topless women....? You know you might get a bit tired in the season if you have to make out with every topless woman."

Glen was frantically trying to tidy up the mess in the flat before she noticed.

"I think you're enough for me at the moment Louise."

She poured out their drinks, as he came back into the room she offered him the glass. He took it and they stood together a moment eyeing each other, tasting the wine.

Glen moved a little closer, their heads nuzzling each other, his hands gently running through her hair. She responded to his touch, moving closer, their bodies touching, the warmth darting between them.

She held his face between her hands and kissed him, gently, then brushing her lips across his cheeks until his passions rose to a frenzy, their bodies entwined and their mouths met in a passionate endless kiss.

Louise pulled at Glen's belt, her hands sliding inside to his crotch.

She took off his shorts, pushing him playfully backwards onto the bed. She had stopped giggling, now she was deadly serious. Removing what was left of her clothes she sat on top off his thighs, kissing his arms, his chest, his neck. Glen pulled her over him, her hair and then her breasts falling into his face. He pulled her down on him, his lips and tongue covering her breasts with kisses, then rolling her over he grabbed her thighs and pushed his penis up inside her and held her tight so that she couldn't move.

She started laughing again and they both laughed, moving now, feeling the power within them, touching and moving, urgently craving but lingering within the moments passion.

She lay entranced as his finger tips gently brushed her neck and he kissed her breasts again and again, and still his penis was pushing up and down within her. She cried out as the first tremors rippled through her thighs. No! she didn't want it to end. She didn't want to feel so vulnerable. She struggled to stop it but the movement only exited her more. Animal instinct took over her body and she craved and cried and shook, squeezing him in a vice like grip, her nails clawing at his back as she arched herself upward.

Their mouths joined, inseparable in their passion, her breathing became deeper and deeper, she groaned, hypnotised by the waves of pleasure that seemed to flow endlessly. The juices flowed from their mouths like rabid animals, pouring into each others jaws, running down their faces. They drank each others passion, sucking the drops from the skin, draining and loving within until his lips touched her nipples. She broke into a frenzy, crying out, begging him to come. He held her tightly as he powered up the last few strokes and they locked together, releasing all the joy and frustration. Their minds drifting into a timeless space for a moment that seemed to last for hours.

Then she cried.

She cried as she'd never cried before. Without control she sobbed into his shoulder, still holding him to her. She was so sad she just couldn't tell him how she felt and then she was so happy she laughed herself to tears.

"I'm sorry, she said, "I just get so emotional sometimes."

She cried again," I don't know what's wrong with me. Just drunk I suppose. Drunk but happy."

"It doesn't matter," he said softly," It's all right."

He kissed her lovingly on the cheek and she smiled. It **was** alright, she felt comfortable with him.

He kissed and licked the tears off her cheek.

And so they spent the afternoon, the evening and the night, caressing each other.

There was a strange whirring and buzzing noise.

The bedroom had the curtains drawn making it difficult to see the source of the noise.

Somebody stirred in the bed.

Although there are two people in the bed, they are both out of sight below the duvet.

The buzzing and whirring continues.

From below the duvet a muffled voice sleepily emerges.

"What the bloody hell is that noise." It was a female voice.

There was no reply.

The heads bob as a dig in the ribs is dispatched.

"What _is_ that noise?"

"It's the printer," Glen replies. "Go back to sleep."

The printer rattles on churning out sheet after sheet of paper. The computer attached to it has been casually dumped on the floor in the midst of a pile of clothes and cardboard boxes.

The printer which is precariously positioned on top of a suitcase falls into a mound of paper, chugs for a while and then stops.

They sleep on.

It was a week later and Glen was still working at Louise's house.

" Do you think this needs another coat ? " he paused for a while, roller in hand, stepping back to look at his art work with the exaggerated analysis of a true artist.

"No, it seems okay, don't you think?" Louise walked round behind him giving him a friendly squeeze.

"I guess." Glen had lost interest in the decorating since his relationship with Louise had taken off.

"We could go out riding this afternoon if you like." Louise sensed his disinterest.

"I'd like that but I've got to do a couple of hours work back at the flat first." Glen started to clear up, " I promised to sort out some programs sometime today."

He left. They would meet up later at the stables.

Louise was busy in the kitchen planning out a special meal for Glen later that night. She had been to the shops and bought enough food for a week, she couldn't decide exactly what she wanted so she bought a huge selection for her to choose from later.

Now it was later and she still couldn't decide.

"Maybe I'm trying too hard," she thought to herself.

There was a knock at the door. She opened it to find two extremely unsavoury looking salesmen.

"I'm not interested," she said abruptly, closing the door.

"Mrs Darcy ? " One of them enquired.

"Yes," she replied impatiently with the door still shut.

"We're friends of your husbands...
Mr Metcalfe and Mr Brandon......"

"Well what is it ?" Louise re-opened the door.

"I wonder if we could come inside for a chat ?"

"No. Just tell me what it is you want," Louise was a little more polite but not apologetic.

"Well it's like this dear,...."

Louise hated his familiarity

"Your hubby, our mate Darcy, owes us some money for a job we did for him."

Then the other one spoke, " and he said, that we could get the money back from you."

"He said nothing of the sort!" Louise flared up." He would have told me first! "

The two men looked at each other.

"Well, let's put it like this then.....
We'd like to take out a loan ...."

The other one interrupted, "for old time's sake."

"...and if you know what's good for you, you'll pay up."

"Piss off!" Louise finally lost patience and slammed the door in their faces. She ran into the bedroom where she kept a small black pistol. Loading it and carefully removing the safety catch she went back to the front door.

She peaked through the side window and was relieved to

see them walking away down the drive.

She watched to make sure they did actually leave, waiting for the sound of their car as they drove off and then picked up the phone and dialled.

"Mr Finlay please. It's Mrs Darcy." She waited for the secretary to put her through.

"Mr Finlay ? Yes I'm very well, and you ?

Yes. I have a message for Frank, can you deliver it for me?

Begin, 'Please confirm loan arrangement to Metcalfe and Brandon,' end. Okay?

"You have some trouble, Mrs Darcy,"enquired Mr Finlay.

"I don't think so, not yet anyway." Louise put the phone down and stared at the wall for a while worrying.

She returned the gun to it's hiding place and continued with the meal.

Not feeling as happy as she had when she started, she opted for a meal out.

The stables were a few miles out of town on the road to Seville.

Glen managed to get a lift from the bar manager who was on his way to pick up some stock from the wholesaler.

" You like to ride?" The manager chatted as he drove, swinging the car erratically round the bends.

Glen couldn't believe his name was really Pedro. " Yes. It's been a long time but I expect I'll get the hang of it again."

Pedro left him outside a derelict farmhouse, he pointed down the track at the side, " Follow your nose! " He laughed insanely and drove off into the dust.

Glen took the track past the farmhouse, in through a large wooden gate and, by following the muck on the track, found his way to the courtyard. It was cobbled, surrounded on three sides by old farm buildings which had been converted into about twenty stables, all with their own doors.

He walked into a large barn at the end and found another twenty or so stalls inside.

"Can I help you Sir?" The voice was huskily familiar but the pseudo-Spanish accent ?

He turned round. It was Louise.

" Oh it's you! "he laughed and they hugged. He sensed some apprehension but let it pass.

"I don't see any horses? " Glen walked beside her, his arm around her shoulders.

"They're all in the field, Michaela has gone to get them, come and have a look."

They walked out of the building and down the country lane at the back. The trees lined the path, the sunlight streaking mystically through the archway of branches.

Glen looked at Louise, her face a picture of radiance, pity he didn't have a camera, he thought.

Walking on further they went through a wood and then into the open air. Suddenly they could see for miles, like the pampas lands of Mexico, the view stretched, as if forever, into the haze in the distance.

The horses roamed free scattered across the dusty grasslands, some with their heads bowed as they rummaged for food.

In the distance, a rider was returning with two horses in tow.

As they came nearer it was possible to see that it was a woman, apparently riding bareback and without the use of reigns, though the horses she was trailing had head tackle on.

"It's Michaela,"said Louise.

The horses were tied to the fence and the saddles put on.

Louise helped Glen to get on." You have ridden before haven't you?"

Glen started to feel a little apprehensive." Yes... but it was a long time ago."

Louise smoothly mounted her horse and reigned it back into immediate control.

They rode of, waving goodbye to Michaela, straight into a canter down the gentle slope of the field and across the sun-baked grasslands.

Glen was beginning to realise that this was not the kind of riding that he was used to. That this was not the kind of horse he had ridden before.

This was not the old nag that routinely plods it's way, twice a day, out of the ordinary English hire stable. Tired, bored, having to be forced into moving it's hulk down the same old route day after day.

This was something new. This horse was not only alive and healthy, it was a pulsing gyrating ton of savage flesh.

He held on to the reigns, trying to pull back the head to stop but could only just about managed to stay upright.

He tried to find the rhythm of the horse and not bounce in the saddle but found he had to half stand in the stirrups to avoid being shaken off.

Louise was streaking ahead, the wind in her hair, the adrenalin rushing through her veins as the horse pounded onward.

It was then that Glen saw they were coming to the edge of the field and that Louise was not turning her horse to go round.

It was then that Glen saw the gate and started to realise the imminent situation.

It was then that Glen saw and realised.

The realisation was, that this horse was a jumper, and Glen wasn't.

The fear started to roll inside his stomach, he pulled hard back on the reigns but nothing happened.

He watched as Louise, in front of him, executed a perfect jump; sleek, within pace, low over the gate, showing great experience and style.

Glen considered kicking off the stirrups and jumping off but he was going too fast. At the last second he pulled the horses head hard to one side and turned him away. Much to his surprise and relief they were safe.

Glen trotted round in a figure of eight to regain control over the horse, or was it to conceal his terror.

He padded up to the gate and leant over to open it.

Louise was a few hundred yards ahead waiting.

She rode back. " I'm sorry, I got a bit carried away then.

I forgot you were a bit rusty."

"Oh that's okay," said Glen, mildly understating his feelings.

They proceeded at walking pace down a track which continued across the middle of the fields to a small river.

They dismounted, Glen still shaking inside from his ordeal.

The horses drank from the stream as they sat in the shade of a tree and talked about their lives, the pleasures and the pain.

The sound of a truck engine broke through the isolation of the moment. Some reckless driver was scattering birds and cattle as he churned a four wheel drive vehicle across the brow of the hill.

It was a jeep with two men in it. One of them appeared to be holding a hunting rifle.

Louise turned pale. " Time we headed back."

She mounted her horse and rode off leaving Glen watching the jeep as it rolled to a halt about half a mile away. They seemed to be using binoculars.

Glen rode off after Louise, luckily he had left the gate open so he didn't have to go through that trauma again.

The horse was tiring a little now as it pounded up the slight gradient. He started to feel his confidence coming back, he even started to enjoy himself.

A shot rang out, he looked behind and saw the jeep across the other side of the river, still a good mile away.

They must be shooting game, he thought to himself.

Louise was already rubbing her horse down when he got back to the stables. He thought she looked shaken.

" You okay ? " he put his arm around her and squeezed.

" Yeah, fine, " she didn't really sound fine.

" I'm going back to town now, do you want a lift ? "

" Thanks." Glen pulled the saddle off the horse and wiped the sweat off it's back.

" You can leave the tackle there, Michaela will put it away later."

Glen couldn't quite see what the hurry was but Louise had already started the engine and was ready to go.

" What's the hurry, " he asked.

" There's some things I've got to do before the shops shut," Louise explained unconvincingly.

He let it pass.

Harry was in the bar.

Glen walked up beside him and ordered a beer.

"You look tanned?" Harry noticed that there was more than a healthy sun tan showing on Glen's face but he didn't pursue it.

"You still working up there, making me loads of dosh then Glen?"

"Yeah. It's nearly finished now, just the glossing to do." Glen sipped his beer watched by Harry who was still trying to work out the change in appearance.

"How did you get on with Louise?" Harry's interest was deepening. He looked at Glen's shoulders which were not in their usual alcoholic slouch, in fact he seemed to have quite a confident stance.

Harry bought another drink for them both.

" Well ? How did you get on with Louise?" Harry pushed for a reply.

" Okay. " Glen was non committal.

Harry talked on about work." There's a new club opening in the town centre, I'm trying to get the painting contract. You interested ? "

"Not really." One weeks painting was quite enough for Glen.

" I've managed to get a computer sent over from England and I'm doing some work for my old firm."

Harry stared at the wall. Another plan up the spout. He had so many problems getting labour, nobody wanted to work any more.

He didn't seem to notice that he was one of them.

Glen was waiting outside on the bar porch where he had spent his first night in Algeciras. His mind was calmer now. It seemed like an age since he arrived on that old beaten up bus.

Louise drove up in her Suburu estate, characteristically late but looking breathtaking in a svelte evening dress.

" You look like a million dollars," Glen was obviously taken aback. " Where were you thinking of going tonight ? I haven't got any other clothes."

" It's alright, they'll take you as they find you. It's your money they're interested in, not your suit. " Louise was occasionally very cutting with the glib remarks.

She felt good. It had been a long time since she had been out on the town and she appreciated Glen's company, not to mention his rugged good looks. Even when Darcy had been around he'd never taken her out much, he'd always been to busy with "the boys" or gambling.

They were ushered into the restaurant, it was Italian though the waiters were a mixture of nationalities. The table was in a suitably secluded corner. The waiter leaned over to light the candle between them. Glen watched the flickering light as it spread over Louise's face giving her an entrancing mystical sophistication. He thought of some of his past relationships and wondered frivolously what trap this femme fatale would spring.

" It's an impressive place," Glen tried to break the ice, Louise seemed lost in her thoughts for a while.

" Have you been here before ? "

" Only once." Louise held back the rest of the sentence, that it had been with her husband, the night before he was extradited back to England.

They perused the menu and started on some fine Italian wine.

" I feel quite close to you," Glen tried again.

Louise reached out for his hand and clasped it tightly." I know."

She was strangely reticent.

" Do you still love your husband ? " Glen was starting to get mildly irritated by the lack of response.

" No. Not for years. It was a bit of a mistake really. I thought he was somebody else."

" Pardon ? "

" I mean, he wasn't the person I thought he was." Louise finally started to open up. " After a while, all his good points turned out to be an illusion and all his bad points were real.

I turned a blind eye to it in the beginning but now I just can't."

She stared into her glass, swirling what was left of the wine around the rim.

" And you ? "

Glen had felt so calm but now he flustered and was lost for words.

" I had a painful marriage. I spent a lot of time pretending everything was okay and buried myself in my work.

We got stagnant, nothing moved, I just couldn't see a way out.

One day I just upped and left.

I never thought I'd have the strength to do it but in the end there was no other choice."

The chef came over with the menu.

" Good evening Madam, Sir, welcome to the Bella Vista the finest restaurant in Spain where we serve the best food in Europe."

Glen thought the chef was exaggerating slightly, " Surely you mean the best food in Spain ? "

" To call my cooking the best food in Spain is a great insult. I am the best chef in Europe, but please, let me demonstrate to you how I have spent my life in the pursuit of culinary perfection. It would be a great honour for me to order for you and then you would be assured of the creme de la creme."

" Okay, but no fish for me, " Louise replied in a matter of fact way.

" And Sir ? "

" No fish."

The chef walked off with a wild flourish of his tea towel.

Louise looked at Glen, " I hope we're going to get some peace and quiet tonight. I fancied a calm romantic interlude. "

" And me." Glen refilled Louise's glass. " He doesn't seem very Italian or even Spanish come to that."

" I heard he was Swedish."

" That explains a lot."

The starter arrived and Glen began to probe Louise's defences again.

" You don't have to disclose anything you don't want to Louise but I am interested in you, and therefore, I wondered about your husband, I mean, how come he leaves you alone so much ? "

Louise remained silent for a while, finishing her starter and then sipping the wine.

She looked at him in a loving way, reaching again for his hand.

" Life is very complicated, it has not turned out the way I would choose. It would be nice if we could have a relationship that was simple but I suppose that would be too naive of me. "

He waited, she had still not answered.

Her legs reached out under the table and wrapped themselves around his.

" I did not tell you before because I didn't know how you would react, even now I am taking a chance, it is not something I want known, you understand ? "

Glen nodded, how bad could it be for christ's sake'

She spoke quietly, her head tilted towards him.

" My husband is a criminal, he is in jail in England." She looked at him watching for a reaction. " He won't be released for at least ten years. "

He looked at her not really wanting to believe it. He started to feel a bit sick. He'd been a fool to think that things were going to work out. Things were never that simple were they, there's always a bit of reality to spoil the dream.

The main course passed him by. They ordered more wine and then hit the brandy. They laughed at each others jokes, teased each other like old friends, and clinched on the dance floor like lovers in heat. But inside, they both felt the fear. The fear that it was over.

That Louise was trapped and could never be free.

Morning broke. Blindingly bright it pierced through the open curtains. He turned to shield his eyes from the glare and was surprised to find himself alone and in his flat.

His hangover gave witness to the excitement of the night before. Some food would make him feel better.

He hazily started to recall the conversations of the night before, thought awhile and then decided to talk to Louise and apologise for his invasion of her privacy.

There was no reply.

Louise had left the restaurant in a flurry of temper.

What the hell did he expect ! Bloody typical, another dominant male trying to surrogate his territory.

She stomped off down to her car but was grabbed from behind and dragged screaming into a side street.

A hand was placed over her mouth as she struggled to get free.

"Shut the fuck up or I'll knock you out, bitch ! "

She was bundled into a car and driven at speed off into the darkness.

She sat in the back of the car sandwiched between two men. She caught a glimpse of their faces in the flash of a car's headlights, it was Brandon and Metcalfe.

"So what do think you're doing ? " She turned to Brandon unable to contain her distaste.

"This," he said with a menacing smile, " is an invitation to a party."

They entered the club by the back door. Louise decided to walk rather than be dragged.

Brandon sat her down in a chair in the office and closed the door. The two men were now seated on desk tops.

" I was hoping to get your attention last time we called Mrs Darcy, but it didn't seem to have any affect." It was Brandon doing the talking.

"Did we frighten you and your friend when you were out riding ?"

Louise looked up at Brandon and stared him hard in the eyes.   " You'll pay for this ! When Darcy hears about this, you're dead."

" Quite possibly, my dear, but then at the moment, you're here," said Metcalfe.

" And he's over there, " laughed Brandon.

He grabbed her handbag and tipped it out over the desk top beside him. He searched through her purse and scattered her makeup all over the floor.

" All we want," Brandon moved around behind her." All we want, is a bit of co-operation." He put both his hands on her bare shoulders. She struggled to get free but he was too strong.

His hands caressed her neck threateningly, tightly gripping her

throat and then releasing.

" It doesn't have to be painful."

"Oh why not ? "interrupted Metcalfe, " I do enjoy a bit of pain. Especially on a tart."

" No," said Brandon slowly and in a controlled voice, " it doesn't have to be painful, but we'd prefer it if it was. " He laughed at his little joke.

Louise was starting to feel that she was in the company of imbeciles. She tried to bluff it out.

" There's no way I'm going to help you."

The reaction was fast. Suddenly the chair was kicked from under her, her coat was pulled back over her shoulders pinning her arms behind her and she lay on the floor with Brandon's knife at her throat.

" One more crap remark like that Louise and I'm gonna let Benny here do a number on you."

Metcalfe's eyes started to glisten with pleasure at the thought.

" Okay. What is it you want." Louise had had enough, she just wanted to get out in one piece.

" You get us some money. You get us £50,000 and you get it tomorrow."

" I ca.. " Louise was stopped mid sentence by Brandon's hand round her throat, his knife slashing at her dress.

" Okay. Okay. ..I'll do it." Louise was shaking with fear.

" You stay here tonight. You go with us to your bank in the morning. You give us the money and we'll let you live.Okay ? "

Glen rang her again at about eleven o'clock in the morning.   Still no reply.

algeciras 5, page 22.

" I've been calling you all morning, can I meet you for lunch ?" Glen finally managed to get through to Louise on the phone.

" Sorry, I'm a bit tied up at the moment, can we leave it 'til later." Louise sounded tense. She was wondering how long she would be able to stall him, he was bound to sense that something was wrong.

It was dark inside the club. A haze of cigarette smoke rose up to the spotlights in the ceiling shooting pinpoints of light down to the floor.

The music pounded in the background, the deep thump of the drums reverberating around the room from the direction of the dance floor.

A couple were entwined in a deep embrace as they gently swayed to the beat. They were unaware of anyone else or the prolific display of colours streaking over them as they danced.

There were tables in front of the stage, mostly empty, a female dancer on stage gyrating graphically with next to nothing on.

Harry sat at the bar, drink in hand, cigarette in mouth.

His eyes had adjusted to the darkness now and he could make out the pool table over the far side where people were extravagantly laying bets with heated debate.

A waitress came up to him. " Can I help you Sir."

" No thanks dear, I'm waiting to see the boss."

Harry shifted his gaze to follow her as she walked back across the room.

" Great looker isn't she ? " It was Brandon. " She only started this week but she's doing fine. "

" She's very young," Harry pondered awhile.

" Yeah yeah." Brandon didn't care how old they were as long as they were cheap and hungry.

" So did you work out the quotation for the refurbishment Harry ? "

" Well, " Harry hesitated, " yes I did. It depends really on whether you're going to use the colours available or if you want special tones, also whether you want the best quality paint or not."

" Just give me the price Harry." Brandon was getting irritated.

" Well it's a about three thousand pounds."

" Okay, put it in writing and I'll let you know within a week."

Harry shuffled with pleasure. " Great, yeah, that's great Mr Brandon."

" Have a drink on the house, " Brandon put his hand on Harry's shoulder and signalled to the barman to refill his glass.

" Don't mind if I do," smiled Harry settling down for a good nights drinking. This could be the place to be, he thought.

Metcalfe came through from the front door looking harassed and walked up to the bar.

He stood next to Harry but didn't speak.

" Give me a short, Ben. No make it a double."

Harry turned to strike up a conversation with him but Brandon came back.

" Everything okay ? " Brandon looked him up and down and didn't like what he saw.

" No." Metcalfe swallowed down the whole glassful and ordered another.

" What do you mean, no." Brandon looked and waited for an answer. " I lost it." Hewitt was still shaking.

" You'd better come in the office." Brandon half dragged Metcalfe out through a side door and into the office.

" What the fuck happened."

" I took the boat over to Morocco, like you said, I saw the guy at the Hotel and bought the dope."

" So what went wrong ? " Brandon settled down into his chair.

" I was coming back in the boat when I got stopped by the Moroccan coastguard. "

" Yes. And. "

" They searched the boat and found the drugs."

" Well what a surprise. It was probably their drugs that you just bought.
I still don't see the problem, they know what's going on anyway."

Metcalf took another big swallow from his glass.

" The problem was, they wanted a thousand dollars to release the boat."

" So you paid them ? " Brandon was getting quieter and quieter.

" I didn't have any money left. I spent it all on the drugs. "

" So you gave them a cut."

" I offered them a cut. But they took the lot."

" I can't believe I'm hearing this. Your supposed to be a crook and you get ripped off by the police." Brandon sagged into his chair.

" We're lucky it was only fifty thousand. " Metcalfe was trying to see the bright side of it.

" And your life. " Brandon spoke in a flat tone.

" Why do you say that ? " Metcalfe nervously looked at Brandon.

" Because the guys we were selling the dope to are here, tonight."

He pointed through the glass of the one way mirror which allowed them to keep an eye on the customers.

There, at the bar, were two extremely mean ex-army types, tall, fit and heavy.

" Are you going to tell them ? " Brandon looked at

Metcalfe and waited for a reply.

" We can tell them a story, " Metcalfe suggested.

" You can tell them a story, " Brandon wiped his brow, " and it had better be a good one. "

" What's the big deal anyway. "

" It's an investment." Brandon explained.

" It's not the drugs they're after, they just want the profit to finance another operation."

" So who are they ? " Metcalfe hesitated.

" They're mercenaries. I don't want to know who they are. They're just mercenaries. So you go and tell them a story, go on."

" You'd better invite them in. "

" I just fancied a day out that's all. "

Louise enjoyed driving and the chance to open up the Suburu on the Autoroute.

" It's great to shop in Gibraltar as well, it's like being back in Bond Street... Well nearly. "

The sun in her eyes, the wind in her hair and Glen by her side. Louise was trying to shake off the bad memories of the last few days and get back to enjoying life again.

She and Glen had sorted out their differences and decided to make the best of the time they had together.

As they drove through the border Glen looked at the airport.

It was strange remembering that not long ago he had flown in here in so much turmoil. It seemed a long time ago now.

" Just in time for an early lunch, " Louise parked and they walked into the town centre arm in arm.

Glen appreciated having a beautiful woman on his arm and he found her exciting to be with, hypnotising and stimulating.

They spotted a pizza bar and both headed in.

It was peculiar to see an English bobby on the beat again.   Most of the shop assistants appeared to be Spanish.

Louise noticed Brandon's jeep cruising down the road and shivered a bit. It's all in the past now , she thought to herself.

They hit the shops after lunch. Louise being an insatiable shopaholic had to visit every store and try on as many dresses as possible.

Glen needed some new clothes badly, not having really bothered to buy anything but the bare essentials since he had been in Spain.

Louise helped him chose, she had a good eye for men's clothes and new what would suit him.

They drove up to the hills behind the town where the

infamous monkeys run wild and later visited the cavern within the rock itself.

They spent the early evening on the beach terrace of the Atlantic Hotel and watched the sun slowly sinking in the west.

" I think we ought to stay ? " Louise was still full of energy even after a full day.

" We could eat here, " she enthused, " We could book in here for the night. It's obviously not very busy at the moment."

" That's a great idea, Louise, " Glen laughed, " all we've got to do is put all our shopping in a suitcase and we'll look like real tourists. " He laughed again, " No, it'll be good. I wish I'd thought of that myself. What would I do without you."

" There's an answer to that," Louise said teasingly.

They booked in and dressed up in the new clothes which they had bought.

Looking at each other they laughed. There they were like an old married couple getting ready for dinner.

The room was warm and cosy for a hotel, Louise ran over her makeup in the bathroom and was just making the final touches when Glen put his arms around her from behind. She turned and kissed him, melting into his arms. The passions rose and they suddenly found themselves involved in more indulgent pleasures than food.

" But I'm so hungry, " said Glen. " I think I'll order some food on room service. What would you like ? "

"Yoghurt, passion fruit, avocado, bananas, chocolate ice cream, wine and more wine. " Louise thought for a while. " And oysters.

Glen looked at her puzzled for a while and then realized.

" Anything to eat ? " he asked tritely.

" Oh don't be so boring, I just want to eat you. " Louise laughed biting at his ear as he tried to order the meal over the phone.

" I don't know what they're going to make of that. "

Louise moved her hands over his neck muscles, squeezing gently in a massaging action. " I expect their used to it. "

Glen got up, dimmed the lights and tried to tune the radio in to some soft music.

" I bought this beautiful kimono, shall I put it on ?

Glen turned momentarily. " Seems like a good idea, "

Louise disappeared into the bathroom to change.

She came back after a few minutes looking stunning in a slinky silk (satin?) Kimono.

She bent down in front of Glen revealing her cleavage as she reached for her wine glass. " Anything I can do for you Sir ? " she enquired, in the manner of a true Geisha.

" Well I wouldn't mind a massage, if you would be so kind ? "

" Certainly Sir. If you would remove your shirt and trousers and lie on your stomach. " Glen obliged.

Louise ran her fingers through his hair and down his back, then manipulated the skin around his shoulder blades.

" A little tension around here Sir, I shall have to spend some time on this. "

" Spend as long as you like, I love all this attention. "

Glen started to relax and feel the warmth circulating as her hands pulled hard on his shoulder muscles.

He drifted off for a few moments as she moved down

over his back and then to his thighs. Hazily his thoughts floated away as he drifted in and out of consciousness.

" Over on your back now please Sir, and you can remove your boxers now. We're not shy now are we Sir ? "

He wasn't shy. He was practically unconscious. Hypnotised or mesmerised, but he wasn't shy.

" Anything special for you Sir, " Louise was starting to feel the power that she had over him. " How about some wine. "

She poured it over his stomach, running her fingers through the pool and spreading it. She sipped and licked a little, her tongue lapping the folds of skin and chasing the drips.

Glen was totally relaxed and calm. " Is it alright if I just lay here, it feels so good. "

" That's alright Sir, " said Louise in her husky voice, " I'll wake you when I need you. I'm just amusing myself for the moment. "

She spread wine liberally over more of his body and put the bottle to his lips so he could drink.

" I think I'm getting a bit sozzled. " She slurred putting the bottle clumsily down.

Her hands surrounded his penis. Moving tenderly from end to end. She kissed it with affection again and again until she took it into her mouth slowly teasingly between her lips, licking and
kissing.

Glen started to groan, his thighs moving responsively to her touch.
Suddenly she could wait no longer. The control and the delight
gone as the animal passion seized at her loins.
She opened her Kimono and swept on top of him kissing him, feeling him, squeezing his body with all the force she could muster.
He lay still, receptive, awake and sensual. Feeling every breath, every touch and every movement she made.
He watched her as she slid over his penis and held herself high above him her, beautiful breasts swaying tantalisingly as she gyrated to orgasm and collapsed on him, breathless and squeezing his arms.
" You bastard, " she puffed, " you bastard. You never even moved. you let me do the whole thing. "
Glen just smiled sweetly, holding her close, feeling her warmth."

After resting for some time he rolled from under her and put his hands gently on her back.
" And now it's my turn, " he said.

They ate the food, spreading it over each other, giggling like children, and then licking it off.
Their bodies were taught with exertion, running with sweat and heat and juice. Their mouths pouring kisses onto each others lips, the drops of juice drooling off their tongues.
The animal cries searching, sobbing, begging.
The craving driving them on to new heights of intensity.
The obsession fanning their hunger, spreading their dreams of surrender to pure emotional response without fear of deception.
Desire, fervour and emotion drowning in their yearnings.

They lay in the jacuzzi for the rest of the night. Embracing and caressing and then falling exhausted into a shallow sleep only to wake up again revitalised and hungry for more passion.

It was three days after their visit to Gibraltar.

They spent the day on the beach at Algeciras soaking up the warmth of the early summer sun.

Soon the tourists would be flocking through the town and over the beaches, but now they still had most of the beach to themselves.

In the cooling evening shade they sat outside the Pescado restaurant sampling the various bite sized snacks and the Sangria, talking avidly about anything that came into their heads.

They were happy in themselves, isolated from the problems of the world and the chores of everyday commerce.

As night wore on they wandered down the main street to the Siske hotel where there was always room for people to let their hair down and dance through the night.

It was like a dream for Glen, he hardly dared pinch himself for fear of waking up.

Louise, who had spent many nights in the hotspots of London, Los Angeles and Rome, found the simple life in Algeciras a welcome retreat from the shallow superficiality of the fast lane.

Pretence used to be everything on her life. The perfect home, the perfect wife, the perfect hostess to her husbands guests, but it was all a fraud. She was almost pleased when the whole lot came crashing down, although it was rather unfortunate that her husband had landed up in jail.

They danced, locked in each others arms, swaying gently to the music. Louise pulled Glen close to her, feeling the love and the warmth between them, she tenderly nibbled at his neck and then froze. In horror she saw the faces of her two assailants, Metcalfe and Brandon standing at the edge of the dance floor, watching their every move.

" What's the matter ? " Glen wondered why Louise had suddenly stopped dancing.

" Oh I fancy another drink, " Louise flushed and made

for the bar.

" What's the matter ? " Glen persisted.

"I have to go, " Louise said abruptly, " I can't explain now. I'm sorry. "

As she walked off toward the exit Glen noticed two men follow her out. He thought he'd seen them somewhere before, but couldn't quite place them.

He realised Louise had left her jacket with her house keys in it,

swiftly finishing off his drink, he left the hotel.

He walked back towards the centre of town, trying to work out which way Louise would have gone. In the distance he caught sight of a zebra styled jeep screeching out of a side street with what appeared to be Louise struggling in the back.

They were gone before he could even think of what to do.

His thoughts rushed for a while, where had he seen that jeep before and then he remembered, it was when they were out horse riding and later he had seen it outside Paco's bar when Harry had been talking to some men about painting the Mayfair club.

" That was it. The mayfair club. " he thought.

It didn't take long for him to get to the club and he was relieved to see the zebra jeep sitting outside the back door.

He paid his money at the entrance and walked slowly into the dimly lit club.

It was packed. He moved through the crowds looking for Louise but after going round the outside of the room several times he realised she wasn't there and started to look for a door out to the offices.

The floor show was just beginning and as all eyes were on the erotic dancers he was able to slip un-noticed through a door marked 'private.'

Behind the door he found a small dark corridor which he followed. The sound of the music faded behind him, he saw lights up ahead and could hear muffled voices.

He moved toward them.

" For God's sake no." It was Louise screaming, pleading.

Glen waited no longer, he smashed open the door to see Louise and the two men. Without a second thought he laid into the two men flooring one with his first blow and then beating the other into submission.

He grabbed Louise and dragged her out of the office, down the corridor, out through the door into the club.

They mingled with the other customers, cautiously making their way to the entrance. Two vicious looking soldiers were coming into the club. Glen avoided them by moving slowly along the wall on the opposite side of the room. They concealed themselves behind the pillars and tried to mix in with the crowd.

Eventually they reached the entrance. The doormen looked as if they had been alerted. Glen back-tracked into the club, searching the darkness. As they skirted the walls he found a fire exit which they opened and quickly slammed shut.

" The door was alarmed, " Glen shouted to Louise, " We'll have to move fast."

They darted through the pathways linking the streets until, a few streets away, they found a taxi to take them home.

At Louise's house they sat silent for a while trying to comprehend the situation. She made some coffee and offered it to Glen.

" I think it's about time you told me what's going on. "
Glen stirred the coffee and looked at Louise.

Louise spoke slowly and cautiously.

" I thought I'd got rid of them. They asked me for some money about a month ago. I refused at first, but they got heavy so I paid them off."

" And now they want more ? " Glen asked. " How much did you give them ? "

" About fifty thousand." Louise was quiet and withdrawn.

"Pounds ! ? "

" Yes. "

" They must have seen you coming." Glen was incredulous. " Why didn't you go to the police ? "

" I couldn't, " Louise paused while she sipped at her coffee. She was calculating how much to tell Glen.

" I haven't been exactly honest with you, " Louise began to divulge. " My husband built up quite a considerable fortune from his criminal activities."

" I gathered that." Glen sat waiting for the rest.

" And I used to look after it for him ," she paused, " and I still am.

" Louise looked directly at Glen. " I'm the front for his legitimate business investments. "

Glen still looked as if he didn't fully understand.

" I launder his illegal profits into stocks and shares."

Glen sat silent for a while stirring his coffee thoughtfully.

" So you're sitting on millions ? "

The enormity of the situation slowly began to dawn.

Right at that moment all hell broke loose.

Two windows smashed, sending flying glass all over the room.

Two mercenaries in camouflage flak jackets and brandishing automatic weapons burst through the broken glass and pinned Glen and Louise to the floor.

Louise was screaming hysterically, the mercenary kicked her to shut her up. Glen struggled to help but received a blow from the rifle butt knocking him into unconsciousness.

When he awoke he was tied up in a chair, the blood oozing down his neck.

Louise sat in a chair opposite to him looking rumpled, crushed and dejected.

" Are you alright ? " She was concerned that she had involved Glen in her problems.

" A bit of a headache that's all. " Glen looked around the room.

Brandon and Metcalfe had joined the two mercenaries. They were making themselves at home, raiding the larder and the fridge for food and drink.

" What's happening ? " Glen leaned over towards Louise trying to keep his voice out of earshot.

" They're taking me to the bank in the morning, they want a hundred grand this time." Louise settled back into her chair. " I've got no choice. "

Glen looked at the automatic rifles casually slung over the mercenaries' shoulders. " Yes. I see what you mean. "

They spent an uncomfortable night in the chairs, torn between fitful sleep and the fear of what might happen tomorrow.

The morning broke early, with fear dawning as their minds awoke to the realities of their situation.

Metcalfe came in from one of the bedrooms.

" I had a lovely nights sleep, " he grinned. " Very comfortable."

He put the kettle on and made himself some toast.

" Nice place you've got here Louise."

Louise refused to be drawn into an answer.

Brandon shuffled in. " Isn't it about time we got going, " he asked Metcalfe.

" No. The banks aren't open yet." Metcalfe had this unfortunate way of making every sentence sound sinister.

They waited until ten and then Metcalfe and Brandon took Louise off to the bank leaving Glen with the two mercenaries.

" There's no need to suffer, " one of them said to Glen. " Make yourself some breakfast, " he undid Glen's ropes. " If you try anything you'll be dead before you hit the ground, "

Glen had no intention of trying anything.

The phone rang, it was Brandon.

" We have to go to the harbour."

The mercenaries pointed to the door, concealing their weapons under their coats.

Glen was starting to get a bad feeling about this. He didn't want to go to the harbour.

They drove on to the quay and waited for the others to arrive.

Glen looked around for some sign of help but there was none.

The harbour was quiet at this point with only a few fishermen tending their nets and the sound of the gentle lapping of the waves against the quayside.

He saw Brandon, Metcalf and Louise leave their car over the other side and walk round to them. They continued walking passed and on to a boat tied up in front of them.

The mercenaries waited and watched to make sure there was no-one following.

The boat engines roared into life with the throaty splutter of a racing car.

" Right, let's get going then." The mercenary pushed Glen hard in the back, forcing him out of the car.

Glen looked at the boat. It looked like an old Torpedo boat from the second world war.

As they cruised out of the harbour Glen and Louise were taken below and locked in a cabin.

They could only hear the roar of the engines, the muffled shouts of the men and the sounds of the sea as they crashed through the waves.

Glen held Louise in his arms.

" I'm sorry. I'm sorry, " she sobbed. " It's all my fault. "

Glen comforted her, " It's all right. "

They sat silently wondering what was going on.

" They've got the money then have they ? " Glen pondered.

" Yes." Louise was unusually quiet.

" So where do you think we're going ? " His hand moved over to hold hers.

" Could be Morocco, Tangier probably." Louise looked out the porthole.

Glen joined her, " Drugs I suppose."

" And then what ? "

There was a silence as they both looked at each other.

The boat powered on across the waterway between Algeciras and North Africa. It was only a matter of an hour before the sound of the engines dropped to a low hum as they slowed down to enter port.

On deck the four men dismantled the heavy shark rods they used to confuse any watchful eyes.

Metcalfe waved to the police on the deck of the coastguard boat as they lazily stretched out sunning themselves.

" Bastards, " he said still smiling. " I bet their high on our dope. "

" They won't get way with that again, " said the mercenary.

When the boat docked, Brandon and Metcalf left to arrange for the pickup.

They were back within the hour and headed out to sea again.

They hadn't gone far along the coast when the engines slowed and then stopped.

The boat rolled gently in the swell as they waited.

Glen and Louise listened as a boat approached and then came along side. They felt the bump as it tied up, the two boats wallowing in the waves and the solid crack as the cases they were loading hit the deck.

There was a lot of enthusiastic shouting as the loading continued and then silence until the engines started up again.

Glen was getting fed up with being cooped up in the cabin.

" I'm going to have a look around outside, " he said to Louise.

He forced open the cabin door with a steel support from the bed and quietly crept outside.

The noise from the engines was even louder in the corridor so he didn't really have to worry about disturbing anyone.

Some of the boxes had been stored below decks so he broke one open to have a look.
He couldn't believe his eyes. He wasn't quite sure but at a guess he'd say they were missiles.
He replaced the packing and closed the lid carefully.
" I wouldn't bother about that too much Mr Howard ? "
It was Metcalfe standing right behind him.
Glen turned slowly and looked at the hand gun pointing at his head.
" Come on, up on deck. It's time we sorted you out."
Metcalfe jammed the gun hard into Glen's ribs causing him to lurch forward over the boxes. He grabbed at the crow bar lying on top of the cases and swung out viciously at Metcalfe the blow falling hard into the small of the neck. A shot rang out but it missed and Metcalfe fell to the floor screaming in agony.
Louise came out of the cabin at the same time as the mercenaries arrived. They dragged Glen and Louise up on deck. Metcalfe limped up behind cursing and screaming.
" He's broken my bloody shoulder. I'll kill the bastard. "
He then proceeded to grab Glen and push him over the side.
" We might as well do it now as later. They know too much anyway."

Glen started to fight back. Struggling with Metcalfe as Brandon made up his mind what to do.

"Okay, ditch them, but get their wallets and I.D.'s off them first." Brandon moved across to Glen and went through his pockets.

Louise started to scream uncontrollably, " You bastards, you'll pay for this. " She clawed frantically at her captors but all in vain.

" There's a ship coming up on the port bow."

One of the mercenaries had noticed a ship on the horizon which seemed to be steaming right for them.

Brandon pointed with his gun, " Okay get them below decks but tie and gag them this time. "

Brandon took the helm, guiding it toward the oncoming vessel and then slowing down to move along side.

Glen and Louise found themselves back in the cabin tied and gagged.

They could hear the ship approaching as the boat languished in the water.

On deck Brandon watched the ship through his binoculars.

" Yes, I think it's our boat. " He seemed quite excited.

As the ship came closer they could see it was a large cargo vessel flying the Libyan flag.

The mercenaries became very tense as it came along side.

The ship towered over them, the heavily tanned Libyan sailors leaning over the railings inquisitively.

A dozen heavily armed scruffs appeared beside them, overlooking the vessel menacingly.

The two mercenaries flinched, holding their weapons ready for use.

From below Glen could hear the shipment being off-loaded again, the bangs and the scrapes echoing through the voids of the boat and the sound of a crane winching.

Again the deep rhythmic surge of the cargo ship's

engines as it pulled away rocking the smaller boat until it's own motor spurted into life pulling it on to an even keel and away across the ocean.

Brandon was ecstatic. " I've been waiting for this moment all my life. " He pulled a bottle of whisky out of the forward locker and gave it to Metcalfe to hold as he went below to find some glasses.

He returned, smiling with joy as he passed the glasses to each of the four in turn and filled them.

" To life ! " he raised his glass with the others.

They sank back into their seats savouring the triumph of the moment.

Brandon lent forward and opened the single case left on the deck. Inside there were wads of notes all carefully packed and wrapped in bank seals.

" Two million pounds, " he said, " not bad for a days work. "

They sat around gleefully passing the money from one to the other

as they finished off the bottle of whisky.

" Just one more job to do, " Metcalfe smiled wickedly, " and then we're off home. "

They threw the glasses in the sea and went below to get Louise and Glen.

Glen shut his eyes from the glare of the sun as he was pushed up on to the deck.

" Take their ropes off, " Brandon said, " it'll look a bit funny if they get washed up bound and gagged. "

Brandon and Metcalf got hold of Glen and started pushing him over the side.

He looked at the sea as it streaked passed the boat's hull the waves curling into an cauldron, he wondered if he had a chance of swimming to the shore, but which direction.

" There's a ship coming. "Glen wasn't sure who said it.

They turned momentarily as another ship passed on the horizon.

" No worry it's too far way, "said Metcalfe.

Glen managed to pull himself upright.

As they turned back around there were three small pops like a bottle being opened.

Glen felt Brandon loosen his grip and then slide to the floor. At the same time Metcalfe's mouth opened wide as if he were to speak but he never did, his knees buckled under him as he slouched to the deck with Brandon and one of the mercenaries.

Glen and Louise stared at the remaining mercenary, his automatic rifle sat on the floor unused, but in his hand was a pistol with a long silencer on the end.

Louise and Glen shook with horror looking at the three bodies, the pinhole pricks in their foreheads starting to emit a dribble of blood.

"Darcy sent me." he spoke to Louise.

"What?" she replied fearful and confused.

"Your husband sent me. To look after you."

They just stared at him bemused, trying to take in what

he was saying.

" You mean you work for my husband ? " Louise tried to understand.

She looked at Glen who was not feeling at all secure in this new found knowledge.

Glen was just about to jump into the sea when he spoke.

"I have no orders on your boyfriend," he paused irritatingly, disinterested in the conversation. " So he's alright. I have no orders," he repeated.

He threw the three bodies over the side of the boat and took it off auto-pilot and turned the bow back to Algeciras.

"But the weapons," said Glen, "missiles? rockets? even nuclear shells? In the hands of terrorists ? "

"I sabotaged them. They're all useless."

He dropped them off at the harbour.

"Put the money back in the bank love," he said giving her a rough half share of the packs of money from the suitcase.

"Thanks," she said faintly, not really knowing whether to be pleased that he had just killed three men for her.

They walked back toward the town centre feeling shocked and speechless. Glen wanted to make some kind of glib remark to break the ice but his throat was too dry from the fear, the sheer terror of the last few hours.

They walked on through the streets and up the hill to Louise's house without a word.

They sat on the hacienda. Louise poured a couple of drinks and they lay back on to the sun loungers.

Staring into the sunset they looked across to the Rock of Gibratar and thought of England, and Frank Darcy.

END